Peppa's Easter Egg Hunt

Published by arrangement with Entertainment One and Ladybird Books, A Penguin Company. This book is based on the TV series *Peppa Pig*. *Peppa Pig* is created by Neville Astley and Mark Baker. Peppa Pig © Astley Baker Davies Ltd/Entertainment One UK Ltd 2003.

All rights reserved. Published by Scholastic Inc., *Publishers since 1920*. SCHOLASTIC and associated logos are trademarks and/or registered trademarks of Scholastic Inc.

ISBN 978-0-545-88130-2

10 9 8 7 6 5 4

Printed in the U.S.A.
First printing 2016
www.peppapig.com

16 17 18 19 20
40

SCHOLASTIC INC.

It is springtime. Peppa is going to do something very exciting today!

Grandpa Pig made an Easter egg hunt for Peppa and her friends. "There are lots of chocolate eggs hidden in the garden," says Grandpa Pig. "Are you ready to find them?"

"Yes, Grandpa Pig!" everyone says.

"Off you go then!" says Grandpa Pig. "But be careful not to step on my plants!"

"We promise to be really careful, Grandpa," says Peppa.

Peppa soon finds an egg hidden in a plant pot.
"I've found one!" shouts Peppa.

Snort!

Rebecca Rabbit finds an
egg under a bush,

and Freddy Fox
finds another in a
wheelbarrow.

Everyone has a chocolate egg except for Richard. "I wonder where the other eggs are?" says Grandpa Pig.

Grandpa Pig puts his hat on Richard's head.
When he picks it up again, a chocolate egg
appears underneath, like magic! Now Richard has
an egg, too.

"So what do we do now, Grandpa Pig?" asks
Rebecca Rabbit.

"You eat your egg, of course!"
laughs Grandpa Pig.

Ha! ha!

"Did you enjoy your Easter egg hunt, children?" asks Granny Pig.

"We found all the chocolate eggs!" says Peppa.

"They're in our tummies now!" adds Freddy Fox.

"Good," says Granny Pig. "Now let's go and see our chickens, Jemima, Sarah, and Neville. They have a special surprise!"

"But they're just boring chickens, Granny," says Peppa. "They're not special." "They have eggs, too, Peppa," says Granny Pig.

"Can we eat them?" asks Freddy Fox.
"No, Freddy!" laughs Granny Pig. "The eggs are about to hatch!"

The baby chicks are hatching. There are three!

Cheep, cheep

"Now that the chicks have hatched, it really is Easter!" says Granny Pig.

Peppa and her friends pretend to be baby chicks.

They all sing:

"I'm a little chick singing cheep, cheep, cheep!
I like to pick up food with my beak, beak, beak!
I've a fluffy yellow head, and some straw for my bed,
And I jump up and down, singing cheep, cheep, cheep!"